For Val, Jet, Guatame, Kali, Grieve, Tiny, Buster, Barky, Islay,
Suzy, Samantha, Ruff, Terrible, Imogen, Lovelace, Lost, Found and Cara.
Thank you for being in our lives. With all our love, now and forever.

BLOOMSBURY CHILDREN'S BOOKS
Bloomsbury Publishing Plc
50 Bedford Square, London, WC1B 3DP, UK

BLOOMSBURY, BLOOMSBURY CHILDREN'S BOOKS and the Diana logo are trademarks of Bloomsbury Publishing Plc

First published in Great Britain in 2019 by Bloomsbury Publishing Plc
This edition published in Great Britain in 2020 by Bloomsbury Publishing Plc

Text and illustrations copyright © Debi Gliori 2019

Debi Gliori has asserted her rights under the Copyright, Designs and Patents Act, 1988,
to be identified as the Author and Illustrator of this work

A catalogue record for this book is available from the British Library

ISBN: HB: 978-1-4088-9303-6; PB: 978-1-4088-9301-2; eBook: 978-1-4088-9302-9

1 3 5 7 9 10 8 6 4 2

Printed and bound in China by Leo Paper Products, Heshan, Guangdong

All papers used by Bloomsbury Publishing Plc are natural, recyclable products from
wood grown in well managed forests. The manufacturing processes
conform to the environmental regulations of the country of origin.

To find out more about our authors and books visit www.bloomsbury.com and sign up for our newsletters

The Bookworm

Debi Gliori

BLOOMSBURY
CHILDREN'S BOOKS
LONDON OXFORD NEW YORK NEW DELHI SYDNEY

"I need a pet," said Max.

"Really?" said Mummy.

"Just a small one," said Max.
"A little puppy?"

"Not a puppy," said Mummy.
"They chew things."

"I need a pet," said Max.

"Mhhmmm?" said Daddy.

"Just a fluffy one," said Max.
"A teeny-weeny kitten. Please?"

"Not a kitten," said Daddy.
"They make the most awful smells."

"A penguin?" said Max.
"It would melt in our warm
house," said Mummy.

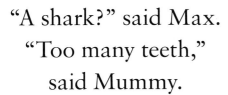

"A shark?" said Max.
"Too many teeth,"
said Mummy.

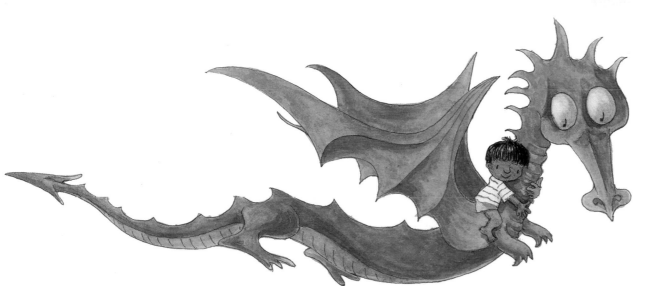

"A dragon?" Max said.
"That would be so cool!"
"Don't be silly," said Daddy.
"Dragons don't exist."

"What about a nice goldfish?"
suggested Mummy.

"No, thank you," said Max.
"Goldfish just swim around
in circles. They're *boring*."

Max decided he would
find a pet for himself.
It wasn't easy . . .

Birds were very chatty, but they
didn't want to live in houses.

Wasps didn't mind living in houses,
but they were very unfriendly.

Flies were *very* friendly, but
they had some revolting habits.

But then Max found a pet
that was just right for him.

"A worm?" said Daddy.
"Ewwww!"

"Just make sure it stays in
your room," said Mummy.
"And look after it."

At first, the worm curled up in its bowl of earth and hid.

It takes time to make friends with a new pet
so Max tried to be patient.

Max sang it songs, stroked its lumpy back and read it bedtime stories. The worm loved stories best of all.

"You're a real bookworm,"
said Max.

In time, Max and the bookworm became the best of friends.
They loved reading books together.

They read that worms
like to eat roots, fruits,
leaves and earth.

But *this* bookworm liked curry and extra hot
chilli crisps most of all. The bookworm *loved* those.

Max noticed that the bookworm was changing colour.
And did the lumps on its back look more like . . . spikes?

Sometimes, when no one was watching, the bookworm
chewed Max's pillow and, sometimes, it made awful smells.

Then, one night, the bookworm sneezed . . .

and smoke began to
pour out of its head.

"Poor you!" wailed Max,
throwing his window open
to let the smoke out . . .

. . . But the bookworm flew out too.
"WOW!" squeaked Max. "You're a dragon! How cool is that?
But don't fly away forever. Come back soon, please?"

Max's dragon flew off into the night
and Max ran downstairs
to tell his parents *all* about it.

"Don't be silly," said Daddy.
"Dragons don't exist."

Max sighed.

"D'you know what?" he said. "I've
changed my mind about having
a goldfish. I'd love one."

Max is very fond of his pet
goldfish . . . although it does
seem to have LOTS of teeth.

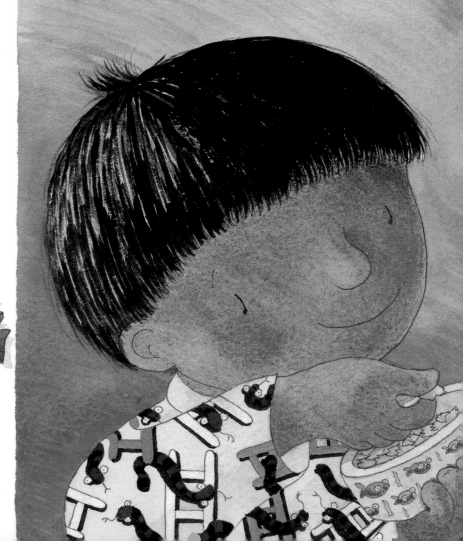

And the bookworm?

It still comes home to visit Max.
Especially when there's
a book at bedtime.